How to Catch an Elf

Adam Wallace

Andy Elkerton

sourcebooks
jabberwocky

It's CHRISTMAS EVE! Hip hip, hooray!

Yes, Santa's coming 'round.

He's bringing toys to girls and boys

in every house in town!

Some kids have tried to catch him,
but Santa's fast, you see!
So they've set their eyes on a smaller prize,
and now they're after *me!*

Now Santa's ready—time to go.

I'm sure your traps are **SCARY!**

I'll do my best to dodge them all

and leave you feeling merry!

In I go, to Emma's house,
to make sure all is clear.
A TINSEL net? Oh, that's just fun!
I won't get caught in here!

Jayden's trap cannot be missed.
I think it's **double-sided!**
He's got his spot on MY naughty list.
You bet *that's* been decided!

Another house is filled with treats.

These kids are getting smarter!

I can't resist the *candy canes.*

My job is getting harder!

Santa slowly lowers me
into a dangerous room.
If I touch down, he won't just frown . . .
there'll be a bonbon BOOM!

SNIP

Your Christmas maze is all laid out.
My work's no longer cushy.
I safely brought you all your gifts,
but, HEY, you ZAPPED my tushy!

And now my radar's PERKING UP!

This next one's quite a chore.

We don't yet know what lies ahead

in this family grocery store.

We run inside and get caught up
in an AVALANCHE of food!
We've seen all kinds of traps before,
but not to this magnitude!

THE *DINNER CANNON*™ burps and spits
and shoots out ham and gravy!
And then it follows with dessert?!
Please, Santa, will you save me?

We tumble down the waterfall
above the eggnog river,
but Santa and I are an **AWESOME** team...

Together, we deliver!

And now it's time for us to leave.

Our night is nearly done.

You tried your best this Christmas Eve,

so . . .

Sourcebooks and the colophon are registered trademarks of Sourcebooks, Inc.

The art was first sketched, then painted digitally with brushes designed by the artist.

Published by Sourcebooks Jabberwocky, an imprint of Sourcebooks, Inc.
P.O. Box 4410, Naperville, Illinois 60567-4410
(630) 961-3900
Fax: (630) 961-2168
sourcebooks.com

The Library of Congress Cataloging-in-Publication data is on file with the publisher.

Source of Production: Phoenix Color, Hagerstown, Maryland, USA
Date of Production: August 2019
Run Number: 5016124

Printed and bound in the United States of America.
PHC 20 19 18 17 16 15 14 13 12 11

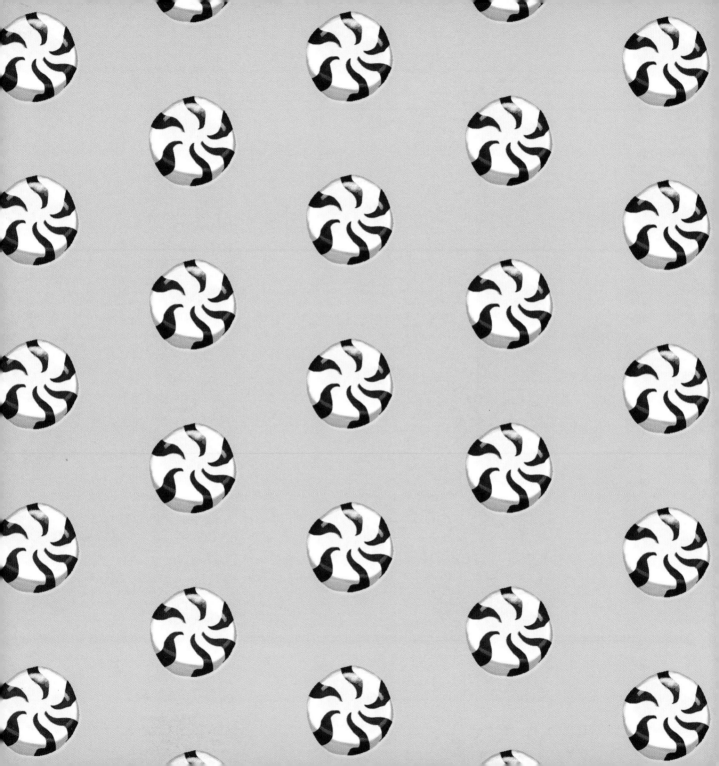